WHAT
SISTERS
DO BEST

BY **Laura Numeroff**

ILLUSTRATED BY **Lynn Munsinger**

chronicle books · san francisco

Sisters can help you

For two great sisters, Emily and Alice . . .
"To there!" —L. N.

For Jessica and Ben —L. M.

Text copyright © 2009 by Laura Numeroff.
Illustrations copyright © 2009 by Lynn Munsinger.
All rights reserved. No part of this book may be reproduced in
any form without written permission from the publisher.

Book design by Natalie Davis.
Typeset in Eureka.
The illustrations in this book were rendered in watercolors,
pen and ink, and pencil.
Manufactured in China.

Library of Congress Cataloging-in-Publication Data available.
ISBN 978-0-8118-6545-6

10 9 8 7 6 5 4 3 2 1

Chronicle Books LLC
680 Second Street, San Francisco, California 94107

www.chroniclekids.com

climb a tree,

push you on a swing,

and share a delicious snack.

Sisters can teach you
how to swim,

do a puzzle with you,

and let you win at tic-tac-toe.

Sisters can teach you
their favorite sport,

start a game of tag,

and show you how
to make a plane.

Sisters can make
music with you,

play pretend,

and help you
build with clay.

Sisters can help you
clean your room,

take you to the library,

and be there
when you need them.

But best of all,
sisters can give you
lots and lots of love!

But best of all,
brothers can give you
lots and lots of love!

and be there when you need them.

take you to the library,

Brothers can help you
clean your room,

and help you build with clay.

play pretend,

Brothers can make
music with you,

and show you how to make a plane.

start a game of tag,

Brothers can teach you
their favorite sport,

and let you win
at tic-tac-toe.

do a puzzle with you,

Brothers can teach you
how to swim,

and share a delicious snack.

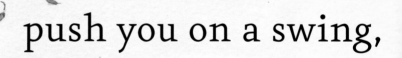

push you on a swing,

climb a tree,

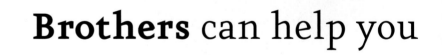

Brothers can help you

WHAT
BROTHERS
DO BEST

BY LAURA NUMEROFF
ILLUSTRATED BY LYNN MUNSINGER

chronicle books · san francisco